Deep in the Forest

Deep in
the Forest

by Brinton Turkle

E. P. Dutton   New York

Library of Congress number 76-21691
ISBN 0-525-44322-3

Published in the United States by E. P. Dutton,
2 Park Avenue, New York, N.Y. 10016,
a division of NAL Penguin Inc.

Published simultaneously in Canada by
Fitzhenry & Whiteside Limited, Toronto

Editor: Ann Durell

Printed in Hong Kong by South China Printing Co.
First Unicorn Edition 1987   W
10 9 8 7 6 5 4 3 2 1